AN INSPECTOR O'REILLY STORY WORDBOOK

The Vanishing Professor

Written by Jack Long

Illustrated by Doug Cushman

CHECKERBOARD PRESS • NEW YORK

The Vanishing Professor

Private investigators Otter O'Reilly and L. Pinkerton were enjoying a cup of tea in their cozy office.

"What a windy day," Pinkerton remarked. "I think it's perfect to fly a kite."

"Eh, what's that?" asked O'Reilly, lost in thought.

"I was saying—" Pinkerton began again.

"Ssh!" whispered O'Reilly. "Either our new shutters are banging in the wind or someone is pounding on our door!"

Suddenly the door flew open. There stood Bella Beaver, wife of the famous professor, Igor Beaver.

"The professor is missing!" cried Mrs. Beaver. "He's vanished into thin air. Please help me find him."

"At your service, madam," O'Reilly assured her. "Now, when and where did you last see the professor?"

"Early this morning in his laboratory," replied Mrs. Beaver.

"Then let us start there and look for clues," said O'Reilly.

satellite

barometer

computer

calculator

077

printer

floppy disk

audio cassette recorder

robot

headphones

string

blueprint

knapsack

fossil footprint

"About nine o'clock this morning," began Mrs. Beaver, as they stood in the professor's cluttered laboratory, "I reminded the professor that the mayor's award ceremony started at noon. Igor said he'd be ready as soon as he finished one more experiment."

"And then?" O'Reilly asked.

Mrs. Beaver sighed. "And then—he disappeared—right into thin air! I couldn't find a trace of him anywhere!"

"Hmmm," said O'Reilly, studying a ball of string he had just picked up. "There are pieces of string all over the place. Oh well, let's look around for some clues."

telescope

retort

battery

glass tubing

scale

flask

test tubes

microscope

laser

eye-
dropper

tweezers

glass
slide

Bunsen
burner

stand

walkie-
talkie

globe

compass

gyroscope

audio
cassette

hammer

protractor

chisel

compass

moon rock

Outside the laboratory door they found another piece of string. There were also footprints on the sandy path leading into the woods.

"Those are Igor's!" cried Mrs. Beaver. "I'd know them anywhere."

They followed the footprints along the path and into the woods. Soon they reached a clearing at the top of a hill. Suddenly the footprints stopped. On the ground lay a pair of scissors.

"Igor's!" exclaimed Mrs. Beaver.

"Forestville is on the other side of the hill," O'Reilly observed. "Maybe someone there will have another clue."

butterfly

evergreens

chimney

roof

hiker

log cabin

camper

lantern

camp fire

tent

sleeping bag

gutter

flashlight

backpack

canoe

fishing pole

frog

duck

pheasant

stoop

rabbit

field mouse

owl

hawk

moose

forest

scissors

path

footprints

mountain

footbridge

quail

fox

stream

waterfall

rocks

blue jay

fir tree

wasps

pinecone

wasps' nest

bluebird

woodpecker

bird's nest

scale

WATERMELON

salami

hot dogs

FRESH FISH

LEMONS

LIMES PEARS

EPPERS

apron

lettuce

apples

oranges

cherries

pineapples

strawberries

PEANUTS

WALNUTS

bananas

COCONUTS

PICKLES

MUFFINS

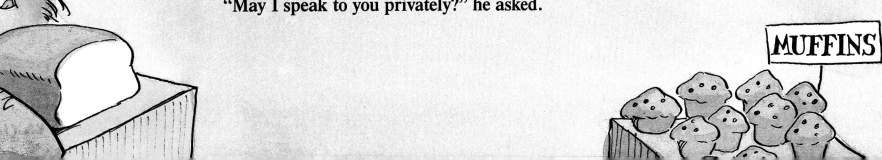

The Forestville general store was bustling with customers. O'Reilly showed his badge to F. W. Fox, the store owner.

"We have a problem," said O'Reilly. "Professor Igor Beaver has disappeared. We hope someone here might have a clue to his whereabouts."

F. W. Fox pounded the counter. "Quiet!" he barked. Inspector O'Reilly informs me that Professor Igor Beaver is missing. Does anyone know anything?"

One of the customers, a certain Squeaky Squirrel, edged up to O'Reilly.

"May I speak to you privately?" he asked.

BANK

DRUG STORE

ART GALLERY

BOOK STORE

THEATER

ticket window

stroller

subway

barber pole

TAXI

roadblock

manhole

barbershop

delivery truck

skateboard

clock tower

pigeon

They all stepped outside.

"I was on my way to the general store," said Squeaky, "when KERPLUNK! This hit me on the head." It was a scrap of paper tied around a big button.

"That's Igor's button!" Mrs. Beaver exclaimed as O'Reilly unfolded the paper. The words *Help! Park!* were scrawled on it.

"To the amusement park, quickly!" said O'Reilly. "The beach is the fastest way to get there!"

bench

SNACK BAR

lifeguard

At the beach, Mrs. Beaver and Pinkerton watched the swimmers. Otter O'Reilly was busy looking for clues. He stopped at the lifeguard's station.

"Anything unusual happen today, Oliver?" O'Reilly asked the guard, who was a young cousin of his.

lifeguard chair

ocean liner

volleyball

net

sandpiper

rubber raft

lobster

sandwich

seaweed

cooler

anchor

guitar

watermelon

suntan lotion

HONEY

iced tea

mustard

sand

potato salad

blanket

"Strange you should ask that, sir," Oliver answered.

"Someone just found this in the water." It was an overcoat, dripping wet.

Mrs. Beaver took one look. "It's the professor's! Oh my! You don't suppose—"

"On to the amusement park," O'Reilly said firmly.

lighthouse

tanker

sea gull

buoy

snorkel

face mask

bathing suit

inner tube

wave

surfboard

horseshoe crab

sand dollar

beach umbrella

starfish

crab

scallop

oyster

clam

sunglasses

pail

beach ball

towel

sand castle

shovel

pennants

top hat

telescope

roller coaster

parachute

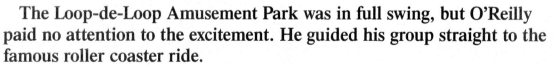

ticket
booth

clown

The Loop-de-Loop Amusement Park was in full swing, but O'Reilly paid no attention to the excitement. He guided his group straight to the famous roller coaster ride.

O'Reilly bought tickets for himself, Mrs. Beaver, and Pinkerton. They climbed aboard, and soon the Loop-de-Loop started up.

"Splendid!" shouted Pinkerton, once they reached the top.

"My collapsible telescope, Pinkerton, if you please," O'Reilly suddenly requested. Off in the distance something was fluttering down through the air. O'Reilly peered through the telescope, then handed it to Mrs. Beaver.

"Why, it's Igor's thinking hat," she said. "He always wore it when he was inventing."

Suddenly Otter O'Reilly shouted out, "Stop this ride! We're at the wrong park. The professor meant *Forestville* Park!"

O'Reilly rushed into crowded Forestville Park muttering to himself. Mrs. Beaver and Pinkerton did their best to keep up.

"Now, let's see," said O'Reilly. "Vanishing footprints, a pair of scissors, and a message from out of the blue, tied to a button."

Pinkerton added, "Don't forget about the coat that fell in the water and the thinking hat. Any ideas?"

O'Reilly looked at Pinkerton. "I'm afraid everything's up in the air," he said. "Everything's – up – in – the – air," O'Reilly repeated slowly. "That's it!" he cried, dancing a little jig.

"Whatever is the matter?" Mrs. Beaver asked excitedly.

"What was the professor's last invention?" O'Reilly asked her.

"Well," said Mrs. Beaver, "it was a special kite that he was working on. Igor dreamed of traveling to outer space."

"Of course!" shouted O'Reilly. "We've been looking for clues on the ground. It's time to look up!"

caterpillar

cardinal

tennis ball

tennis racket

tennis court

jogger

net

chef's hat

bee

fork

picnic basket

barbecue grill

roses

apron

picnic table

picnic bench

tulips

ladybug

grasshopper

radio tower

Whoosh! As O'Reilly, Pinkerton, and Mrs. Beaver looked up, something sailed overhead.

"It's the professor!" said O'Reilly.

"It's Super Beaver!" yelled Pinkerton.

"It's Igor!" Mrs. Beaver corrected.

With a sudden gust of wind, the professor's invention caught in the branches of a very tall tree.

"We'll have you down in a jiffy," O'Reilly called up to the professor.

"When the rockets ignited and I took off, things got a little out of control," the professor called down. "But it was a most exciting trip!"

tunnel

train

smokestacks

derrick

factory

cliff

town

bridge

trailer truck

modern house

riverbank

cottage

river

dock

raft

weeping willow

kayak

tractor

paddle

paintbrush

canvas

palette

rocket

kite

helicopter

windmill

barn

silo

scarecrow

oak tree

crops

tractor loader

bulldozer

mushrooms

frog

snake

turtle

And that is how Otter O'Reilly and his ever-faithful companion
L. Pinkerton solved the mystery of the professor who vanished into
thin air.

At exactly twelve noon that day, Professor Igor Beaver was given a
double award by the mayor of Forestville. On the trophy were the words:

To Our
Best Inventor
and
First Astronaut

The crowd cheered!

"And there's another special award," announced Mayor Minnie
Muskrat. She held up two shining badges. "To Forestville's Finest,"
she read.

She presented the badges to O'Reilly and Pinkerton, and gave
them each a kiss. The crowd shouted, "Hooray! Hooray!" O'Reilly
and Pinkerton blushed happily. It had been a *most* successful case!